SIGGI THE SASQUATCH

Ida & Matthew Kaller-Vincent

Illustrations by Ida Kaller-Vincent

SIGGI THE SASQUATCH

First published in the United States in 2021

ISBN: 978-0-578-83731-4

For Juniper & Oleanna

May your lives be richly diverse

In the deep green forest of the Pacific Northwest,
Sits Siggi the Sasquatch with a lump in his chest.
It is awfully lonely out here in the wild,
He has wanted a friend since he was a child.

Hikers would come to the forest by day,
But when they saw Siggi they scampered away.
Siggi did not know why they were scared,
He just wanted to find someone who cared.

Siggi would cry, showering the forest in tears,
being alone is one of his biggest fears.
He is big ,brown, and furry, but also, sweet, soft and kind,
So, why oh why, is a friend so hard to find.

Rather than sit and wallow and grieve,
The sasquatch decided it was time to leave.
He packed all his things in a little red bag,
And went down a
trail that went zig
and then zag.

After four days of walking past the last lonely tree,
Siggi our Sasquatch found himself at the sea.
He jumped in the water just on a whim,
Luckily, Sasquatches know how to swim!

After swimming real far Siggi stepped on to land,
It was a very hot place full of cacti and sand.
He was covered in fur and sweating a lot,
A place for a sasquatch this surely was not.

He traveled some more and now missed the heat,
Sitting on ice is a very cold seat.
The penguins were friendly, as was Simon the seal,
But Siggi moved on because the cold was unreal.

Siggi escaped the cold and headed northeast,
Now, in every direction was a wonderous beast.
They screeched, rumbled, and trampled the ground,
It turns out Sasquatches aren't the biggest around!

Next, he arrived where it was hot and quite sticky,
Finding friends in this jungle might prove to be tricky.
Things creeped and they slithered and from
the bushes they stared,
"I hope nothing wants to eat me"
Siggi loudly declared.

Leaving the jungle, he went up and over a hill,
The ground turned cold and the air caught a chill.
Siggi looked down and spotted a print in the snow,
Inside him a flicker of hope started to grow.

The print in the snow seemed very new,

So, Siggi climbed up to get a good view.

There in a distance under bright moonlight,

Something was waving, its color was white.

The two of them met in a valley below,
Siggi waved at the creature and said a cautious "Hello".
The creature waved back saying, "My name is Betty".
"I live in the mountains
because I am a Yeti".

Betty looks different from Siggi, that's true,
Her fur is snow-white and her skin is quite blue.
The sasquatch looks foreign to Betty as well,
With his brown shaggy fur and his green forest smell.

To base friendship on color would be a real shame,
Because in reality they are mostly the same.
Despite looking different, each from their own land,
A friendship was sprouting, and that's pretty grand!

Some people approached much to Siggi's delight,
But Betty felt different and got quite a fright.
She started to run, her eyes had grown wide,
She shouted at Siggi "I know where to hide!"

Betty explained, humans often chase her around,
Who knows what would happen if she ever was found.
"They have tiny feet and curly eyelashes,
And run after me with big scary flashes."

But Siggi had noticed these people seemed kind,
So, suddenly, a thought popped into his mind.
What if we are afraid of what we don't know,
Maybe humans are friendly in both forest and snow.

Siggi stood up and stepped out of the cave,
He knew now he had to be brave.
A woman outside smiled and looked very nice,
So, Siggi smiled back to break the ice.

The woman grabbed Siggi and started to run,
"Come meet my friends it will be so much fun!"
To Betty this human still seemed a bit scary,
How can you trust someone who isn't that hairy.

The humans weren't afraid, nor were they frightful,
This meeting of new friends was truly delightful.
It was exciting for Siggi to finally meet,
These people who once ran from his big feet.

Betty, it seems after so many years,

Has finally conquered all of her fears.

A door has opened deep in her heart,

Because of a sasquatch just doing his part.

Sitting down together on the soft forest floor,
None of these creatures afraid anymore.
They talked and they laughed
and shared many things,
And basked in the warmth
that new friendship
brings.

The big furry sasquatch had love all around,
For the places and people he had newly found.
Siggi started this adventure to find something new,
He has now accomplished what he set out to do.

We all come from different places,
With different skin and different faces.
When you meet someone different, it is really no biggie,
Just remember the story of Betty and Siggi.

CPSIA information can be obtained
at www.ICGtesting.com
Printed in the USA
LVHW071939080122
708081LV00006B/71